# Hand Shadows

# Hand Shadows

Susan Wismer

Michele Green

Suzette Sherman

WINTERGREEN
STUDIOS PRESS

**Wintergreen Studios Press**
Township of South Frontenac
21 Cutler Rd., Yarker, ON, Canada K0K 3N0

Photography by David Earle, Michael English, and Michele Green
Book design by Rena Upitis

Composed in Calibri and Gill Sans; typefaces designed by Lucas de Groot and Eric Gill, respectively.

Library and Archives Canada Cataloguing in Publication
Wismer, Susan; Green, Michele; Sherman, Suzette.
Hand Shadows / Susan Wismer, Michele Green, Suzette Sherman.
ISBN: 978-1-989321-28-7
Poetry — General.
I. Title. Hand Shadows.
Legal Deposit — Library and Archives Canada

# Contents

# Hand Shadows: A Collaboration

In the COVID-19 winter of 2020, believing our isolation would soon end, Suzette Sherman and Michele Green of *Passionate Heart—Women's Stories Through Dance* invited me to create a collaborative performance of poetry and dance as part of a series for International Women's Day 2021.

I had previously attended a *Passionate Heart* performance and a writers' workshop with author and facilitator Susan Scott in November 2019 and was familiar with their work. My response to the invitation to collaborate was an enthusiastic *Yes*!

Suzette and Michele, friends for many decades, joined forces in 2017 for a performance at the Guelph Dance Festival. Forty years had passed since they last danced together professionally. The connection they felt as mature dance artists and the way dance had enriched and informed their lives led them to assess what they could contribute to dance moving forward. In lieu of more formal stage performances, they looked for a way to link dance presentations of emotional integrity with small, intimate audiences. *Passionate Heart—Women's Stories through Dance* was created in 2018 and continued until 2023. All performances concluded with an informal discussion where the audience could share their responses to the dances:

> *Each of these dances tells a very simple human story. As women interpreting, we've called them 'women's stories' and indeed they're told from a woman's point of view. But the truth is they offer a theatre of emotions and those feelings are undoubtedly experienced by everyone. (Suzette)*

During the pandemic, Suzette and Michele developed the idea of collaborative performances as part of an effort to increase *Passionate Heart's* audience base by introducing new elements to the program. Reaching out to creative women of various genres proved to be an interesting and stimulating process and one that

1

encouraged audiences to see modern dance from new and multi-layered perspectives.

Shortly after we started our collaboration, the IWD March 2021 performance series was swept aside by a new series of COVID-19 shutdowns. Initially, we thought we might need to delay our performance by a few weeks. Reality was different.

For a nearly a year when pandemic conditions allowed, I travelled to Guelph to watch rehearsals. Suitably masked and distant, I sat in a corner of the dance studio making notes. Some of those notes became poems for this collection. Other notes assisted me to edit and match previously written poems with the feeling and intent of individual danceworks.

All the dances included in *Hand Shadows* were chosen from the existing *Passionate Heart* repertoire. Through discussion, we collectively paired dance with poetry. As we rehearsed various possibilities for the performance program, poems and dances were in conversation, evolving and changing in relationship with one another:

> *The poems had a great influence on how we perceived and performed the dances. In the performances, the poetry preceded the dance and set up a scenario for the audience. Suzette and I moved into that framework to become the character or the emotion the poem evoked. It was an amazing experience to continually fill out the story of the movement. With each collaboration the input made the dances richer and more meaningful. (Michele)*

Three live performances of *Hand Shadows* took place in late 2021 and 2022 with due precautions in place. In all, *Passionate Heart—Women's Stories Through Dance* presented 50 performances. Twelve were collaborations involving writers, poets, musicians, composers, authors, performers, and scholars.

After our first performance of *Hand Shadows* someone suggested we create a book. We discussed the idea and decided to work together on it, not only to document our collaboration, but also to offer to readers a sense of the particular importance of creative arts during times of upheaval, fear, and uncertainty:

> *Through lockdowns and shutdowns and isolation, working with Suzette and Michele was a constant source of inspiration and hope for me and offered a much-needed sense of community. Such good company through those difficult weeks, months and years assisted me to become stronger, braver, more resilient, more creative. I will always be grateful for our collaboration. (Susan)*

Susan Wismer
with Michele Green and Suzette Sherman
September, 2024

---

## Passionate Heart Mission Statement

*Passionate Heart* was born out of our desire to share what we find so compelling about dance, to initiate new audiences to the language of modern dance, and to offer dance as the potent storytelling medium that it is.

We believe the transformative power of this art form can aid in processing emotional experiences in powerful, nonverbal ways, offering healing, comfort or simply a moment of quiet peace in people's fast-paced complex lives.

Suzette Sherman and Michele Green, 2018

I recognize that *Passionate Heart* is poetry of consequence and great beauty.

David Earle

The Dancers and the Poet, November 14, 2021

Jay D Luchsinger

## How to survive a plague

Wipe doorknobs

Wash hands

Wear masks

Maintain distance

Dream

Persist

Repeat

This is it, the art form alive and well—brimming with challenges and rewards.

David Earle in rehearsal with
Michele Green and Suzette Sherman, *Within Walls,*
July, 2018

After all that can't be undone

after warnings, apologies, too little too late,
wildfires, floods, viruses, war

plague still slouching among us

how to find words?

# The Hand Shadows Program[†]

| The Poems[‡] | The Dances |
|---|---|
| **Before** | **Summersong** *(2018)[§]* |
| **Perfection** | *Choreographers: Michele Green, Suzette Sherman* |
| | *Music: Flower Duet from Lakmé by Léo Delibes* |
| | |
| **Epiphany Night** | **The Prisoner** *(2009)* |
| **Hand Shadows** | *Choreographer: David Earle; Dancer: Michele Green* |
| | *Music: Unknown music from the late 1300s* |
| | |
| **Sanctuary** | **Within Walls** *(2018)* |
| **Hourglass** | *Choreographer: David Earle* |
| | *Music: Jeff Bird adapted from Hildegard von Bingen* |
| | |
| **Stories** | **As It Is** *(2007)* |
| **Today's Instructions** | *Choreographer & Dancer: Suzette Sherman* |
| | *Music: The Lord's Prayer by Oliver Schroer* |
| | |
| **Antiphon Ukraine,** | **Waltzing Matilda** *(2021)* |
| **March 2022** | *Based on David Earle's Maelstrom (1996)* |
| **Dresden Cup** | *Music: Christina Macpherson* |
| | *Musician: Michael Thomas* |
| | |
| **Canon for Rehearsal** | **Smile** *(2021)* |
| **Mother's Evening Dance** | *Choreographers: Michele Green, Suzette Sherman* |
| | *Music: Charlie Chaplin* |
| | *Singer: Madelaine Peyroux* |

---

[†] Program performed November 14, 2021, March 13, 2022, Guelph, ON; Clarksburg, ON May 29, 2022
[‡] Poems written and performed by Susan Wismer.
[§] Dates indicate the year of the premier performance of each dancework.

## Before

Summer wind through lavender's dusked leaves
garden gate boards weathered grey
the house finch's long song soars
from crabapple tree branches
dark nimbus clouds scud
swift off the lake

Before
thunder and rain
send us running
to garden tools
laundry lines
windows

Held
in the cup of my hand
your knuckles, blue-veined
small knobs of arthritis at the joints
a breath—

                        clasped palms.

# Perfection

Each earthbound globe
an unseen adventurer
in the underland, welcoming
this spring's raised bed—

moist soil *friable*, worms' tender reach
delicate root threads grow, stretch
descend

We can't be too careful with courage
with joy

To keep each small living creature
intact, naked, fearless: two heart-shaped leaves
a hint of red bulb, white net of rootlets
clustered in the cup of one hand, small plants

in a tangle of seedlings, slow explorations
of separation, thinned, moistened
returned to waiting soil

In the welcoming breath
of this only day

a promise of rain, misted brush cool
on my sleep-warmed cheeks, ferns push
tight curls out of earth, becoming

We can't be too careful with what falters
with loss

My weary hands plunge into dirt,
fingertips cautiously probe, touch tendrils,
new shoots, what returns
every Spring

in the morning, damp soil, small radishes—
perfection.

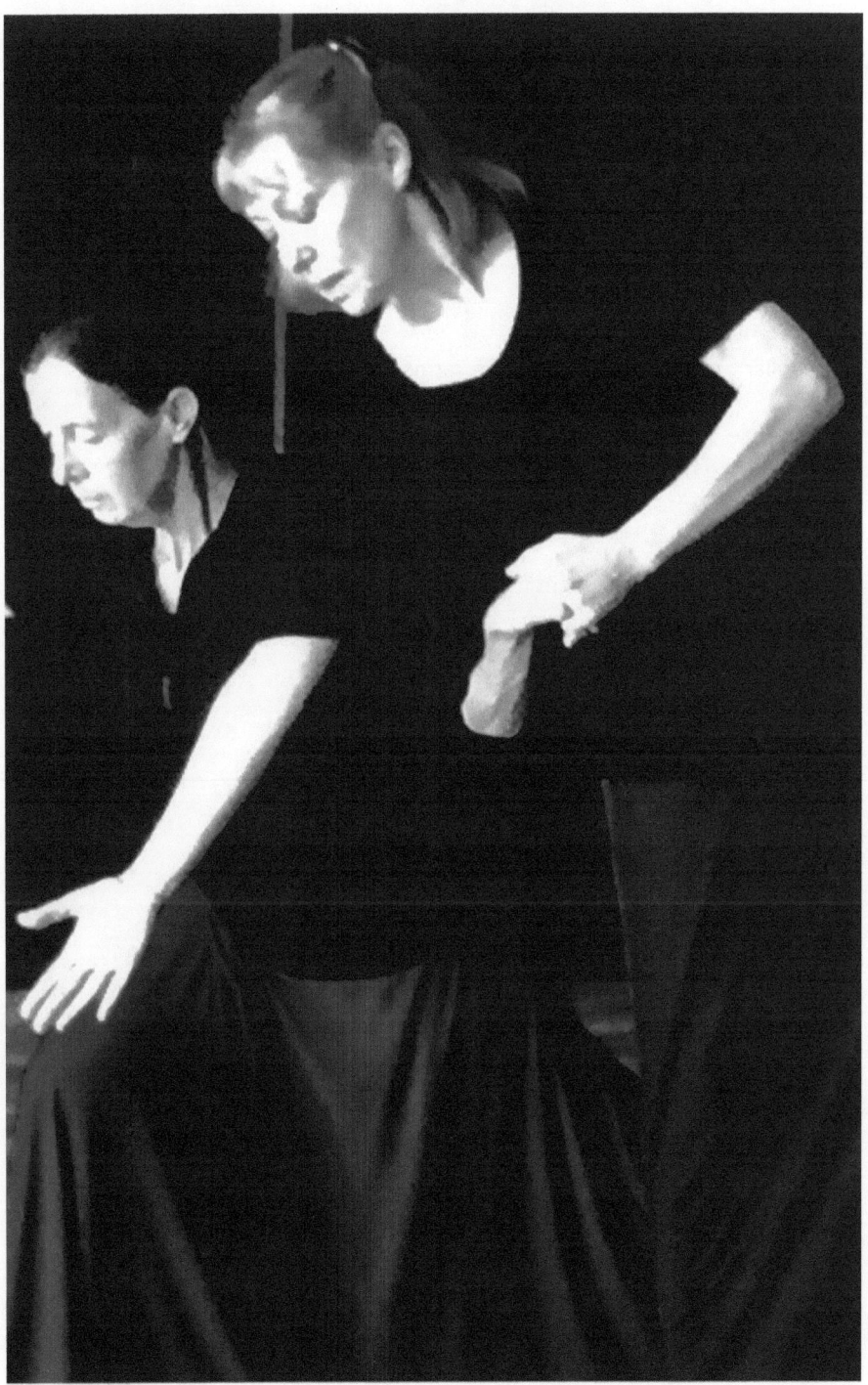

# Epiphany Night

*South Frontenac County, January 6<sup>th</sup>, 2020*

Profuse, celestial
       falling

       stellar   obsidian skies   we were   arms flung   faces raised
                  mouths filled with wind
whirling
high over trees

shape-shifted creatures of night fired light
raven black wings, silver manes

       sharp shining hooves

we returned

almost       too late.
       to remember
              we are human

                     descending

                            from stars

## Hand Shadows

Imprisoned
bound hands, cuffed wrists
fingers clenched and outstretched—
clenched again.

The bagpipe's nine notes hearken limits
of scale, of breath
in the keen cuts
of grief.

Sun stripes the barred window
at the wall her fingers draw
chiaroscuro, shadow
and light.

Silent
butterflies
flight.

## Sanctuary

nettles, scotch thistle, dame's rocket, chickweed
wild lettuce, blue clouds of forget-me-not
unkempt in my garden

sun stencilled sumac, warm scent
of lilac, loamed shade under maples
one toad

my trowel furrows, digs deep
in this life I fear, world peace
will not come

regardless, unasked
the wood fern
uncurls

## Hourglass

sand drifts

through the narrowed waist
of my dreaming

mirrored
our bodies unfurl
blurred, blended, softened

time steadfast, falling
a long coil of red ribbon unspools

reflection, glass walls
what might have been

fine-grained, passing
beloved, the dusting
of years

## Stories

what toes have to say
about wings, about
angels daring
to ask

all that the face
holds untold, rising
wordless as feathers
to carry

stretched foot, outreached arm
quiet face, your crooked elbow
raised— a practice
of flying

stories, stories
still seen

     when the drummers go home
     when the dancers are gone

in the soft smudge of feet
on the floor

## Today's Instructions

1.
Celebrate this—
There is no escape.


2.
As if this day
the world ends
because
        maybe

it already has
    come—

Hold my hand.


3.
We are still here.

## Antiphon Ukraine, March 2022

A telling, tolling
resounding, repeated
insistent

on the dark wounds of earth
marked refusing, resistant
plangent

for singing, dance, stories
as rest for the ear, quiet
remembering

each unheard voice

over and under
the boom thrust of war
and exploding
every insensible bomb.

Antiphon for silence
endurance, peace.

# Dresden Cup

*Poland* 1943

Found
by the roadside
three cups and three saucers

spare beauties of smooth rounded shape
some hesitant hand
brushed paint    over porcelain
a blue rise of lines    along curve across lip

horns of a ram
fern tendrils rising in spring
soft curls at the back
of a young daughter's head

She carried them with her
all through that war
scalpel and morphine
her doctor-hands bloodied
sirens    Red Cross    ambulances    stretchers

her children in Canada    safe    so little
could be

saved

*England* 1945

What endures is by chance
the fragile

made sacred
by circumstance
                          three saucers
                  three cups




*Canada* 2021

I want

hot black tea, this Dresden cup
warm in my hands, steam pearling the air

          to imagine

the artist lifts a cup to the light
          tips brush to paint
                    places one final dot
                          below each tender curl.

In a world where so much is going haywire, you two dance and there is something right in the universe. The emotion deepens every time I see this.

Audience member

## Canon for Rehearsal

*Temple Studios, Guelph*


wicking light

                                  beneath piano, below drumbeats

a shadowed thrum

                                  strong toes spread wide

supple feet of the dancers

                                  grip of broad umbered oak planks

gold swaths of afternoon sun

                                  glide, crossing the floor

through tall windows, lifting

                                  child voices, laughter

grey limestone church

                                  twin spired spines rise

contrapuntal.

Guelph Youth Dance Studio
Rehearsal and performance space

# Mother's Evening Dance

*Holding the small silver opening up to the light*

Black thread measured
nosetip to armstretch, three quick turns
around forefinger, roll of the thumb makes a knot, then
chestnut curls at the back of her neck jump
to the snap of snipping front teeth. Lips
and tongue moisten one end, before
deftly she slips in the thread, trace
of a red lipstick shine: Revlon, *Fire and Ice.*

*Under the lamp*
*in small lifts and falls,*
*shadows*

On her lap, fabric—
cut, patch and stitch, green, yellow, brown. Tomato
pin cushion, lamplit moving thread, shining needle moves
through holed elbows, gaped knees, ripped sleeves, until
weary with gathering all that is torn
into her hands, she stands and turns,
leaves what remains
unrepaired, for
tomorrow

*One arm's upward*
*bend, reach of her hand,*
*twist of a wrist, the lamp switch's click.*

*Darkened room.*

## Resilience

Is collaboration
the quiet sinew of resilience?  Perhaps
its heart. A flexible resistance—
pulmonary, pulsing.

To sing, dance, continue. To insist.

Susan Wismer

Michele Green

Suzette Sherman

# Acknowledgements

*For the Earth*

There have been and there are injustices all over the world. Many of us are here in Canada because our ancestors were forced to flee homelands, leaving places and people they loved, hoping for a better life for their descendants. As settlers and immigrants, we are guests on the ancestral lands of many Indigenous Nations.

We acknowledge and hold ourselves accountable to the spirit of care and of friendship that is the foundation of all of the original treaties and covenants.

We cannot change the past but we can change the present. If we all breathe a little deeper, open our hearts a little more, this world will be a more just, compassionate, and humane home for us all.

*For the People*

*Passionate Heart* was created in collaboration with Dancetheatre David Earle. We, all three of us, want to thank DtDE for its ongoing support.

All photos were created and/or edited by David Earle, Michael English, and Michele Green. The sketch *The Dancers and the Poet* was created by Jay Luchsinger during the November 2021 performance of *Hand Shadows* and is used with permission.

Thanks to James Green and Glenn Sherman for their support. That three performances went smoothly during challenging times was due in significant part to their practiced and multi-faceted assistance.

We are grateful to Guelph Youth Dance for studio rehearsal and performance support. Many of the poems in the collection were first drafted during rehearsals and practice sessions in this studio. We are grateful as well to Marsh Street Theatre in Clarksburg, Ontario for hosting the South Georgian Bay performance, and to all the audience members in Guelph and Clarksburg who willingly put on masks and sat at a distance from one another at our three performances.

A special thanks to Wintergreen Studios Press for your enthusiasm and willingness in taking on this book project.

Earlier versions of some poems have appeared in other publications: Dresden Cup is at www.CollingWords.ca, the website of the Collingwood Poet Laureate; Canon for Rehearsal is in *Leap: Poems in Memory of Leslie Strutt* (League of Canadian Poets Chapbooks, 2022), Today's Instructions appears in *Pink Flamingos* (Wintergreen Studios Press chapbook series, 2022), Perfection has been published in *Spike: Poems in a Time of Pestilence* (Cannon's Creek Press, 2021) and, along with Antiphon Ukraine in *Poems in Response to Peril* (Pendas Productions/Flying Raven, 2022). Sanctuary was featured by the League of Canadian Poets in *Poetry Pause* (October 25, 2022). Poems from this collection will also appear in *Hag Dances,* forthcoming from At Bay Press, 2025.

Post-Performance (L to R): Michele Green, Susan Wismer, Suzette Sherman

**Susan Wismer** (she/they) wrote a first poem at age 5 — a misspelled outpouring of yearning for a pet dog. Writing has been a passion ever since. She is grateful to live with two human partners and a very large dog on the southern shore of Manidoo-gitchigami (Georgian Bay) in Ontario. www.susanwismer.com

Born and raised in Chicago, **Suzette Sherman** began training with Stone-Camryn School of Ballet, continuing her studies in New York City. Her career includes two years apprenticing with Winnipeg Contemporary Dancers and one year performing with Saskatchewan Dance Theatre. Suzette then joined Toronto Dance Theatre and for nineteen years toured worldwide dancing major roles. Since its inception, Suzette has been a principal dancer with Dancetheatre David Earle. A teacher throughout her career, Suzette is proud to work closely with David Earle teaching his technique and repertoire. Suzette has appeared in several film and television productions. Currently continuing teaching and performing, she is exploring a newer creative voice in choreography.

**Michele Green** began her professional dance with Winnipeg Contemporary Dancers (1971–1973). She co-founded Saskatchewan Dance Theatre with husband, Jim Green and former teacher Lusia Pavlychenko (1973–1976). In 1980, Michele, Jim and their two children moved to Stouffville, Ontario where she opened The DanceCentre, successfully teaching until retiring twenty years later. Turning her sights to writing, Michele worked for a decade as a feature writer for *In The Hills* magazine. In 2006 Dance Collection Danse Press published her book *David Earle, A Choreographic Biography*. Now a grandmother to four beautiful grandchildren, Michele is thrilled to have the opportunity to return to dance.

It occurred to me how radical it is, in this time of great sensationalism, to simply perform your dances not much differently than were it a rehearsal. To dance, as friends, in simplicity, because the need to create and to share is present and why deny that? I think this is what I found most moving.

Audience member

We left feeling so inspired

The world looked so powerful and so beautiful ... so true

The poetry opened hearts as well as doors and windows

David Earle

*Wintergreen Studios Press is an independent literary press. It is affiliated with the not-for-profit educational retreat centre, Wintergreen Studios, and supports the work of Wintergreen Studios by publishing works related to education, the arts, and the environment.*

www.wintergreenstudios.com

www.ingramcontent.com/pod-product-compliance
Lightning Source LLC
Chambersburg PA
CBHW032347020726
47499CB00009B/3201